Not Just Second Place

by Tracey E. Dils

HOUGHTON MIFFLIN HARCOURT
School Publishers

Printed in China

ISBN-10: 0-547-25304-4
ISBN-13: 978-0-547-25304-6

16 17 18 19 0940 19 18 17 16
4500569761

Lauren smiled at the kids she passed in the hallway of her new school. The hall was buzzing. Lauren couldn't make out all the words, but she did hear laughter. The school was much smaller than her school in Arizona. Still, it seemed like a friendly place.

Just keep smiling, Lauren told herself. That was the way to make friends.

Lauren had always had a little trouble making friends. She was shy and kept to herself most of the time. But this year, at her new school, she was determined to come out of her shell. But how? She pulled her long brown hair over her ears so that no one could see her small hearing aid. That was one thing she was a little embarrassed about. Then she headed to her new classroom.

After the morning bell, Lauren's teacher introduced Lauren.

This is Lauren," Mrs. Sanchez said. "She's just moved to Woodstock. Lauren, would you like to tell us a little about yourself?"

"Umm. Well, I . . ." Lauren stammered. She felt her face get hot. Then her words came in a rush. "My dad's the new basketball coach at the high school. We moved from Arizona. I have an older brother and . . . " Lauren stopped to catch her breath.

"Welcome, Lauren," Mrs. Sanchez said. Next, her new classmates introduced themselves. Lauren took a sweeping look around the room as each student said his or her name. A girl in the front row gave her a wide smile. Mrs. Sanchez pointed to the empty desk next to the girl and invited Lauren to sit down.

When the lunch bell rang, Lauren learned the girl's name was Meg.

"Let's eat lunch together," Meg said. "The food here is supposedly healthy." Meg rolled her eyes as she said it. Lauren giggled and followed Meg into the hallway.

BASKETBALL TRYOUTS TONIGHT

On the way to the lunchroom, Meg pointed at a sign. "Hey, basketball tryouts are tonight," Meg said. "I bet you are pretty good, your dad being a coach and all."

Lauren just nodded. Actually, she had been one of the leading players on her team in Arizona. But she didn't want to brag about it.

Lauren swallowed hard. "Sure," she said. "A little."

"Great. Then you don't need to be shy!" Meg said. "Anyway, everyone makes it. The tryouts are just to assign people to teams."

Meg smiled. Lauren nodded back.

At tryouts, Lauren realized something. Most of the girls had not played much. They needed to learn the basics, like how to dribble. Of all the girls, Meg was the real beginner.

Lauren knew she had a choice. She could play as well as she could. Or she could play at the same level as the rest of the girls. As much as she wanted to come out of her shell, she wasn't ready just yet. The last thing she wanted to be in her new school was different. Her hearing aid made her feel different enough.

Lauren heard a whistle. The coach waved his arm to tell everyone to sit on the bleachers.

"I'm going to break you into teams," he said. "The Blue Streaks will meet in that corner." He pointed to a far corner of the gym.

"On the Blue Streaks, we'll have Maya, Grace, Caroline, Meg, Katie, Sam, and Lauren."

"All right!" Meg said, smiling at Lauren.

Lauren joined her teammates in the corner. They ran some preliminary drills. Lauren played as well as the other players. She missed a couple of baskets that she probably could have made. She listened to the coach correct her form.

She also saw that Meg was having trouble with dribbling. Lauren knew it was important to keep your head up. Meg looked at her feet instead. One time, her feet got all tangled up and she stumbled.

Lauren knew she could help Meg. She just didn't feel that bold—not yet.

Saturday was their first game. Lauren didn't know what to expect.

When she got to the gym, the team's opponents had arrived. They were warming up. Some of the girls looked pretty good. The Blue Streaks would really need to play hard to win.

"Did you see those girls?" Meg asked her. "They look really good. And they are really tall. It's obvious we're going to lose."

Lauren nodded. "It's not that obvious," Lauren said. "We just need to have a good game."

"Yeah," Meg said. "But most of us barely know how to play."

Lauren thought about what Meg said. Maybe she could give Meg a few tips. And if she played up to her level, maybe they'd have a chance.

"Listen, Meg," Lauren said. "Our team in Arizona was pretty good. Here's one tip they gave us about dribbling. Keep your head up. That way you can see the other players." Lauren passed Meg the ball. "Try it," she said.

Meg tried, but she kept looking at her feet. Lauren said, "No, Meg, look at me."

Meg looked at Lauren. She dribbled the basketball a few times. She was getting a little better! She still looked at her feet every once in a while. "Hey," Meg said, "I'm not so bad at this!"

Lauren nodded. "Let's give these guys our best, okay?" Lauren said when the team huddled.

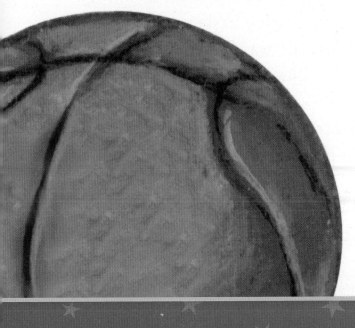

The Blue Streaks were losing by eight points at the end of the first half. During halftime, the coach told the team how well they were playing.

"For this early in the season, you girls had a great first half," he said. "Now let's focus and see if we can beat these guys."

Lauren looked at her teammates. "Let's go!" she shouted. "We can do this."

Caroline, Meg, Maya and Grace looked surprised. This wasn't the quiet and shy Lauren they knew. Even the coach looked surprised.

But the coach yelled back even louder than Lauren had. "That's right, Lauren! Let's do this!"

The Blue Streaks played hard. Lauren showed her real stuff. She made three baskets right away in the second half. Then she was fouled and made two free throws. The Blue Streaks were tied with their opponents.

When the buzzer sounded, the Blue Streaks were down by two points. They hadn't won the game.

"Way to go!" Lauren yelled at the end.

"But we didn't win," Meg said.

"Yeah, but it sure was fun to get that close, wasn't it?"

Meg smiled and nodded. "We'll get them next time!" she said.

In the locker room, the girls all toweled off. It had been a hot and hard game. Lauren pulled her hair up to wash her face. Just as quickly, she let it fall again. But it was too late.

"Hey, Lauren," Caroline said. "What's that in your ear?"

Lauren took a deep breath. She had gone this long without anyone noticing. And now they had. But suddenly, Lauren didn't care. Being shy hadn't worked in basketball. And being shy about her hearing aid probably wouldn't work either.

"I need it to hear," she said. "I have a hearing impairment."

"It sure doesn't slow you down! Especially today," Meg said, giving Lauren a high-five.

Lauren slapped her hand and smiled. She was getting to like this new Lauren.

At the next practice, the coach pulled Lauren aside.

"Lauren," he said, "that must have been some team you played on in Arizona. Do you think you can show our team some of the drills you did?"

"Sure," said Lauren, surprised at how steady her voice sounded.

For the rest of the season, Lauren helped the coach come up with drills. She also helped the rest of the girls with their shooting. By the end of the season, Meg—and the rest of the girls—didn't look like beginners at all.

The Blue Streaks ended up winning second place in the league. The girls were all awarded second-place trophies. For Meg, it was the first time she had ever gotten a trophy. For the other girls, it was the first time they had gone so far in a season.

Lauren had a few first-place trophies from Arizona. She wasn't disappointed in second place, though. This trophy would always mean something very special to her. This trophy was from the year Lauren won second place. It was also the year that Lauren had won something far more important. She had won new friends. And she had learned how good it felt to be herself.

Responding

✔ **TARGET SKILL** **Theme** What do Lauren's thoughts and actions tell you about the theme of the story? What details contribute to the theme? Copy and complete the chart below.

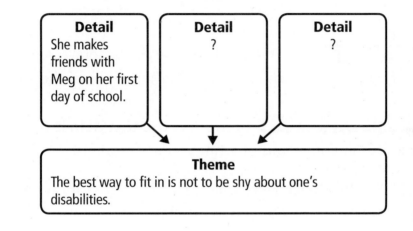

Detail
She makes friends with Meg on her first day of school.

Detail
?

Detail
?

Theme
The best way to fit in is not to be shy about one's disabilities.

Write About It

Text to World A great many people in the world are hearing impaired. What can be done to make their lives easier? Make a poster explaining some of the ways to help the hearing impaired fit in.

TARGET VOCABULARY

brutal	opponents
embarrassed	preliminary
gorgeous	supposedly
obvious	sweeping
officially	typically

TARGET SKILL **Theme** Examine characters' qualities, motives, and actions to recognize the theme of the story.

TARGET STRATEGY Visualize Use text details to form pictures in your mind of what you are reading.

GENRE **Realistic Fiction** is a present-day story with events that could happen in real life.